Who Spilled the Beans?

Story by Joy Cowley
Illustrations by Diana Magnuson

The squeaky mouse spilled the beans.

2

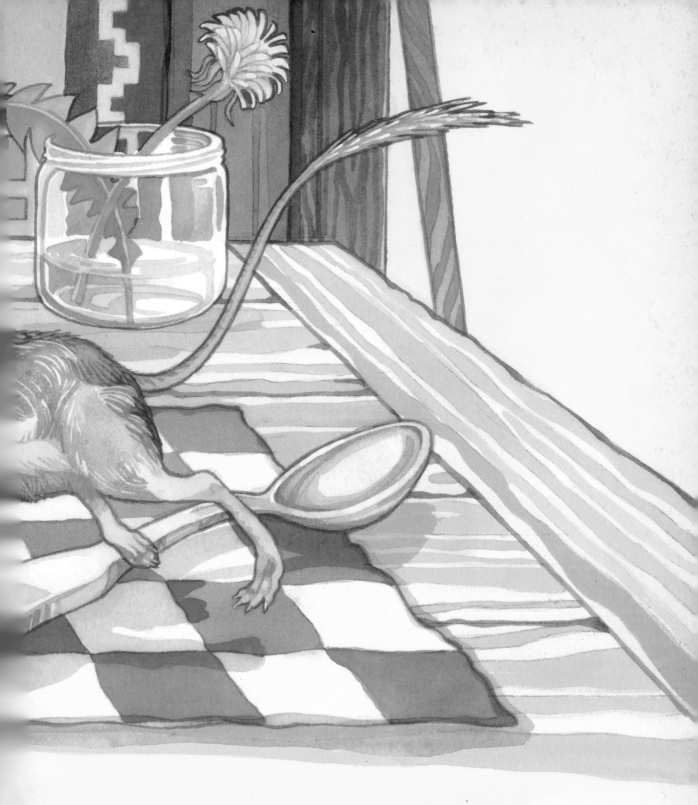

What squeaky mouse?

The squeaky mouse who
ran from the scaredy cat.

What scaredy cat?

The scaredy cat
who ran from the
flappy hen.

What flappy hen?

The flappy hen who ran
from the yelpy dog.

8

What yelpy dog?

The yelpy dog who ran
from the jumpy cook.

10

What jumpy cook?

The jumpy cook who ran
from the big fat greech.

What big fat greech?

**The big fat greech
who came out with a shout.
What shout?**

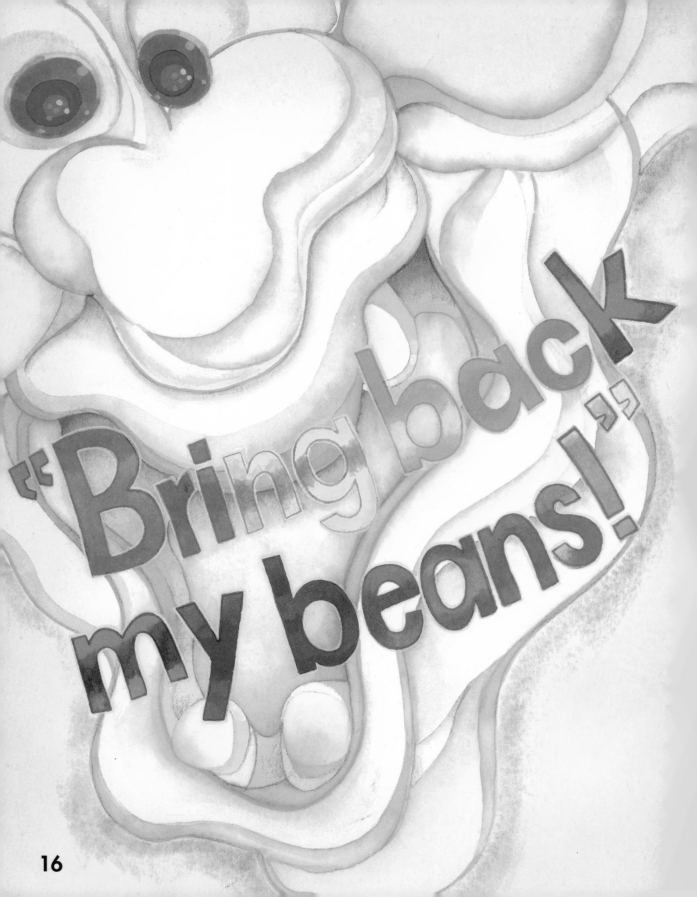